Acting Edition

Clown Bar 2

The Clownening

or

A Bigger Shoe

or

What Ya Gonna Do?

or

Never Trust a Clown

or

Undercover Clowns!

or

The One in Which Happy Gets Popped and No One Knows Who Done It

by Adam Szymkowicz

SAMUEL FRENCH

No one shall make any changes in this title(s) for the purpose of production. No part of this book may be reproduced, stored in a retrieval system, scanned, uploaded, or transmitted in any form, by any means, now known or yet to be invented, including mechanical, electronic, digital, photocopying, recording, videotaping, or otherwise, without the prior written permission of the publisher. No one shall share this title(s), or any part of this title(s), through any social media or file hosting websites.

For all inquiries regarding motion picture, television, online/digital and other media rights, please contact Concord Theatricals Corp.

THIRD-PARTY MATERIALS USE NOTE

Licensees are solely responsible for obtaining formal written permission from copyright owners to use copyrighted third-party materials (e.g., incidental music not provided in connection with a performance license, artworks, logos) in the performance of this play and are strongly cautioned to do so. If no such permission is obtained by the licensee, then the licensee must use only original materials and materials that the licensee owns and controls. Licensees are solely responsible and liable for clearances of all third-party copyrighted materials, and shall indemnify the copyright owners of the play(s) and their licensing agent, Concord Theatricals Corp., against any costs, expenses, losses and liabilities arising from the use of such copyrighted third-party materials by licensees. For music, please contact the appropriate music licensing authority in your territory for the rights to any incidental music not provided in connection with a performance license.

IMPORTANT BILLING AND CREDIT REQUIREMENTS

If you have obtained performance rights to this title, please refer to your licensing agreement for important billing and credit requirements.

CLOWN BAR 2 was originally commissioned by Majestic Repertory Theatre in Las Vegas, Nevada (Troy Heard, Artistic Director), opening on May 12, 2022. The director was Troy Heard, with scenic design by Steve Paladie, lighting design by Marcus Randolph, costume design by Candice Wynants, hair & makeup design by Rowan Morris, sound design by Cory Covell, choreography by Kady Heard, original music by Brandon Scott Grayson, and lyrics by Adam Szymkowicz. The stage manager was Apollo White. The cast, in order of appearance, was as follows:

PETUNIA	Napsugár Hegedűs
MUSTY / GUSTY	Robert Ryan
MAC	Aaron Barry
GLORIA	Diana Martinez
HAPPY MAHONEY	Matt Antonizick
POPO	April Sauline
VIRGINIA / BRIGHAM BILL	Venus Cobb
CLITEAU, CLITEAU / TWINKLES	Angel Mendoza
BILLY BILL	Gabe Gentile
WILLIAMY BILL	Cory Covell

CHARACTERS

Male Clowns

CLITEAU, CLITEAU
TWINKLES
MUSTY
GUSTY

Brigham Bill's Boys

BILLY BILL
WILLIAMY BILL
BRIGHAM BILL – played by the actor who plays Virginia

The Cops

GLORIA
MAC

Lady Clowns

PETUNIA

POPO

VIRGINIA – Perhaps played by the actor who played Bobo in *Clown Bar*. If a male actor, this should be done without artifice in drag.

HOHO – played by a male clown in drag [Billy Bill or Williamy Bill (nonspeaking)]

JELLYB – played by a male clown in drag [Billy Bill or Williamy Bill (nonspeaking)]

The Clown Boss, Deceased

HAPPY MAHONEY

SETTING

The Clown Bar. A bar full of clowns set up like a cabaret. Action takes place in various audience areas and also on the small stage. Audience members are encouraged to dress like clowns. If possible, hand out clown noses to the audience along with their programs. Actors, stagehands, ushers, etc. are all dressed in full clown makeup with bright hair and clown noses. Their outfits could be clowny or like gangsters from the '30s or more recent gangsters. Feel free to make guns as colorful as the clowns. Clowns may hold cliplights to illuminate scenes. Clowns probably haul off the dead too so actors don't have to lie there the whole time.

TIME

About two years after the events of *Clown Bar*. The Clown Bar is rundown now. But look, if you didn't see/read *Clown Bar*, that's fine. You'll still understand the play.

NOTE ON MUSIC

Optional music by composer Brandon Scott Grayson is available for a fee. Licensees should contact their licensing representatives if interested in using this music.

SPECIAL THANKS

Special thanks, in no particular order, to:

Troy and the amazing cast and crew at Majestic.

John and Rhoda Szymkowicz, Seth Glewen, the Gersh Agency, Maggie Toole, Tricia O'Toole, Tish Dace, Kristen Palmer, Wallace Szymkowicz. Elizabeth Bochain. Joe Kraemer.

Amy Rose Marsh, Garrett Anderson, Nate Netzley, Abbie Van Nostrand, Nicole Matte, David Geer, Rebecca Schlossberg, Courtney Kochuba, Rosemary Bucher, and everyone at Concord/Sam French.

At Juilliard, Tanya Barfield, David Lindsey-Abaire, Enid Graham, Charlie Oh, Brittany Fisher, Alex Riad, Stephen Brown, Daniella De Jesús, Lia Romeo, Nick Kaidoo. Evan Yionoulis, Derrick Sanders, Richard Feldman, Kathy Hood, Jerry Shafnisky, Kaitlin Springston, James Gregg, Lindsey Alexander, Hannah Rubenstein, Aly Homminga, Maya Lopez.

Gwydion Suilebhan, the New Play Exchange, and those who left reviews there of this play: Cheryl Bear, Joey Reihart, and Alexandra Bianco.

Kevin Hoffman, Kim Shively, and the students at Elon University. Tommy Truitt, Kenny Harvey, Jack Morrill, Ross Brunschwig, Kelsey Moebius, Balazs David, Hope Nevins, Haley Covington, Markley Bortz, Eduardo Sanchez.

Actors from the reading at Majestic: Bryan Todd, Alex Sund, Richie Villafuerte, Natalie Senecal, Mike Vargovich, Josh Sigal, Tim Cummings, Andrew Young, April Sauline, and Charlie Starling. Thanks to Tessa Raden, Allison Gold, and the Dramatists Guild Fund for the support of that reading.

I'm incredibly grateful to the actors who helped me by performing in development readings of this play.

Daniel Talbott and Addie Johnson, Kip Fagan, Andrew Neisler, Ari Schrier, and everyone at Rising Phoenix and Pipeline who made those first *Clown Bar*s happen.

Everyone (over fifty theaters) who decided doing *Clown Bar*, the first play, was a good idea. Without you, I never would have thought yeah, let's go back to that well and see if there's anything there.

*For Troy Heard. Thank you for your comedic clown genius and for your
enthusiasm and hard work in continuing to build the world.
This play wouldn't exist without you.*

*(At rise, **MUSTY**, a sad clown, has been singing. **PETUNIA** enters. She nods to him and says, "Okay," which means sing the song that starts the play:)*

[MUSIC NO. 01 "THE CLOWNS HAVE ALL GONE HOME"]

PETUNIA. Okay.

MUSTY. Okay. I guess. Well. Here we are again. I see a lot of non-clowns here tonight. You might not wanna be here. Unless you wanna get maimed. Or killed. Or converted to the seedy underground clown crime life. Or killed. Or squirted with seltzer. Or killlllled. Murder-ed. Deadened. Or winked at. Don't say I didn't warn you.

THE BOZOS ALL ARE BOZING
THE AUDIENCE ARE DOZING
LIKE WRESTING A LAUGH FROM A STONE,
THE CLOWNS HAVE ALL GONE HOME

THE BOSOZERS ALL ARE BOOZING
THE LOSERS ALL ARE USING
I THINK I'LL DRINK ALONE
THE CLOWNS HAVE ALL GONE HOME

WHEN PRETENDERS TRY PRETENDING,
THEIR HEARTS THEY ARE MENDING
LET OUT A VIOLENT MOAN
THE CLOWNS HAVE ALL GONE HOME

WHEN THE SHOOTERS ALL ARE SHOOTING
TO SETTLE THEIR DISPUTING,
IT CUTS RIGHT TO THE BONE

BUT THE HOOKERS KEEP ON HOOKING
THE USERS KEEP ON COOKING
AS THEY SAY, WHEN IN ROME
WHEN THE CLOWNS FINISH CLOWNING
AT NIGHT THEY DO THEIR DROWNING
THE CLOWN BAR IS THEIR OWN
THE CLOWNS HAVE ALL COME HOME
THE CLOWNS HAVE ALL COME HOME
THE CLOWNS HAVE ALL COME HOME!

Thank you. Thank you. I'm going to take a quick break.

(Enter **MAC** *and* **GLORIA**, *two plainclothes cops. They pass* **MUSTY** *as they walk in.)*

(Hostile.) I smell hot dogs.

MAC. What? I don't smell hot dogs.

MUSTY. Hot dogs made of pork.

MAC. Oh. A cop joke.

MUSTY. Or like bratwurst... Made of pork.

GLORIA. Aren't you dead? I thought he was dead.

PETUNIA. *(A clown, entering from the back.)* This isn't Dusty. This is Dusty's twin brother, Musty.

GLORIA. Huh. He's pitchy.

MUSTY. I'm not pitchy. You're pitchy! You're pitchy!

PETUNIA. Relax, Musty!

MUSTY. I see you. I know what you are.

GLORIA. Yeah.

MUSTY. I smell meatballs! Made of PORK!!!

(Exit **MUSTY**.*)*

MAC. He could have just said, "I smell bacon." Or "ham."

MUSTY. *(Re-entering and exiting after his line.)* I smell cops! Yeah. Yeah. Yeah.

GLORIA. All right, we're here. Why are we here?

PETUNIA. Shhh. Keep it down.

GLORIA. Where's Twinkles?

PETUNIA. He retired.

MAC. Bottom of the Hudson?

PETUNIA. Witness protection. But you already know that.

GLORIA. Yeah I already know that. But I didn't know if you knowed that.

PETUNIA. I knowed it. We figured you was about to roll on us. But then you never rolled on us.

GLORIA. I'm not at liberty to comment.

PETUNIA. We figured you didn't have the whole picture yet but now the picture's changed.

GLORIA. How's that then?

MAC. What do you want, Petunia?

PETUNIA. I want you to do some investigating. And I don't mean that sexually. Usually I mean that sexually.

GLORIA. What kind of investigating?

PETUNIA. Murder!

MAC. Clown murder? That's not our beat.

PETUNIA. I know. I know. But for old times' sake.

MAC. Whose old times? We don't have old times, you and me.

GLORIA. She means because of Happy.

MAC. What about Happy?

PETUNIA. You was friends, wasn't you? When Happy was a cop too?

MAC. Sure but that's the past. The past is the past.

GLORIA. Petunia, are you saying what I think you're saying?

PETUNIA. Happy's been murdered!!!

>   *(A beat. They take it in, sadly.)*

MAC. It was bound to happen. Clown crime being what it is.

GLORIA. Still. Makes me a bit sad.

MAC. Sure. Sure.

GLORIA. I liked him.

MAC. Sure.

GLORIA. He was a good cop.

MAC. And then he wasn't.

PETUNIA. He was a clown, then a cop then a clown. Now
   he's dead.

MAC. I asked him to come back to the force once.

>   *(Lights change. **HAPPY** enters in a memory.*
>   *Memory music. **HAPPY** is a clown, but maybe*
>   *not as clowny as the other clowns. May wear*
>   *a fedora.)*

Come back to the force, Happy!

HAPPY. No.

>   *(Lights change. **HAPPY** exits.)*

GLORIA. I didn't know you did that.

MAC. Yeah you know. I care.

GLORIA. Yeah.

MAC. I'm complex.

GLORIA. Sure.

MAC. I have depth.

GLORIA. You really do, don't you?

MAC. Deep recesses of depth. I'm a real piece of work. Once you get to know me.

GLORIA. I asked him to come back to the force once too.

MAC. You did?

(Lights change. **HAPPY** *enters in a memory.)*

GLORIA. You're not happy here, Happy.

HAPPY. I know it.

GLORIA. Maybe the clown life's not for you.

HAPPY. Maybe. But what can I do about it?

GLORIA. Just get out. Leave town. Change your name. Or take off the nose and be a cop again.

HAPPY. I think I crossed a line I can't uncross.

GLORIA. I can tell people you were deep undercover all this time.

HAPPY. They won't believe you. Anyway, I can't go back to the beige life now. I'm a clown. Once a clown, always a clown.

GLORIA. Even when you want to be something more?

HAPPY. Nothing is more than a clown. That's the problem.

GLORIA. Come back to the force, Happy.

HAPPY. No. I wish I could. I can't. Stop looking for me. Stop thinking about me.

GLORIA. I can't.

HAPPY. Have you tried? I mean really tried?

GLORIA. It hurts.

HAPPY. We can't talk anymore. I don't want anything to happen to you.

GLORIA. But –

HAPPY. Go.

(Exit **HAPPY.***)*

GLORIA. That was over a year ago.

MAC. I didn't know that. Were you and Happy…

GLORIA. What?

MAC. Close?

GLORIA. I don't know. Is anyone really close in this life?

MAC. Yeah yeah. I know. I meant –

GLORIA. I barely know myself, really. How can I know another? And if you can't really know someone, how close can anyone ever be?

MAC. I meant –

PETUNIA. We all die alone in the end.

MAC. Okay, yeah, but what I mean is –

PETUNIA. He means, was you and Happy fucking?

GLORIA. He doesn't mean that. You don't mean that.

MAC. Uh. Yeah. No. Yeah. No. I wouldn't say something like that.

GLORIA. Yeah. See? He didn't mean that.

PETUNIA. That's what he means.

(Pause. The question lingers.)

GLORIA. And you say he's dead.

PETUNIA. Yup.

GLORIA. Where's the crime scene?

PETUNIA. There's no crime scene.

MAC. Where's the body?

PETUNIA. There's no body.

GLORIA. Then how do you know?

PETUNIA. I just know. He's gone missing.

GLORIA. When was the last time you saw him?

(*Lights change.* **HAPPY** *enters in a memory.*)

PETUNIA. It was Thursday last I think and Happy was low. You okay, Happy?

HAPPY. I'll be fine.

PETUNIA. What's got you down?

HAPPY. Nothing. Nothing. (*Sighs.*)

PETUNIA. Running a clown crime syndicate more difficult than you thought.

HAPPY. It's not that. I mean that's not all of it.

PETUNIA. You thinking about Blinky and how she's dead and how much in love with her you was?

HAPPY. No.

PETUNIA. You thinking about your dead brother, the junky clown who only wanted to be funny?

HAPPY. No. No.

PETUNIA. You thinking about how I'm in love with you but it makes you sad because you don't love me back even though Blinky's long long gone?

HAPPY. What?

PETUNIA. Nothing. Nothing. It's not what you meant.

(*Enter* **POPO**, *a terrifying clown. She is covered in blood and waving around a bloody chainsaw. We're still in the memory.*)

PETUNIA. Hey Popo.

POPO. *(To* **HAPPY.***)* I did that thing you wanted me to do.

(**HAPPY** *nods.* **POPO** *exits.)*

PETUNIA. And that was the last I saw of him.

(Lights change. **HAPPY** *has gone.)*

GLORIA. Okay well first we gotta talk to Popo.

PETUNIA. Sure, yeah but not dressed like that. One of you's gonna have to go undercover.

GLORIA. Go full-clown you mean?

PETUNIA. Half-clown's never done anybody any good.

MAC. I mean I guess I could do it. Or do you want to do it? You want me to do it? I can do it. I can do it.

GLORIA. He's never gone undercover-clown.

PETUNIA. A rookie. I love the rookies. Even the word just makes me shiver! Rookie. *(She shivers.)* Rookie! *(She shivers.)* Let's get some nookie, rookie. You want a cookie, rookie. I'll be Princess Leia, you be a wookie, rookie.

MAC. I'll do it.

GLORIA. Give me a minute with my partner.

(**PETUNIA** *moves away, but maybe not that far away.)*

MAC. Okay, strap me with a wire. I'll go in.

GLORIA. Sure. Yeah. Just. Don't fall for it. Promise me.

MAC. Don't fall for what?

GLORIA. The clown life. I know it can be intoxicating. All that glitter, the fake nose. The laughs. But that's not who you are. Not really. Don't get sucked into it.

MAC. Don't worry about me.

GLORIA. I worry about you. You haven't had a lot of experience with ladies. And the ladies in here are clown ladies.

MAC. They're loose.

GLORIA. I wish there was a looser word than loose. They do anything. Anything! And when they do it, it's funny too.

MAC. What do you mean, anything?

GLORIA. Like I said. Keep your head.

PETUNIA. *(Returning.)* Both of 'em.

> *(Scene change onstage.* **PETUNIA** *exits.* **MUSTY** *comes onstage and starts singing.* **MAC** *and* **GLORIA** *move off to the side. During* **MUSTY**'s *song, we see* **MAC** *become a clown, theatrically, in full view of the audience.)*

[MUSIC NO. 02 "BECOMING A CLOWN"]

MUSTY.
SOMEHOW YOU ALWAYS KNEW
BEFORE YOU EVEN STARTED

THE WAY THAT YOU WHISTLED,
THE WAY THAT YOU FARTED

THE WAY MAMA BRISTLED
WHEN YOU SEEMED CLOWN-HEARTED

THAT'S 'CAUSE YOU'RE
STARTING,
BEGINNING,
BECOMING,

STARTING,
BEGINNING,
BECOMING A CLOWN

THEY SAY TAKE THAT NOSE OFF,

THEY SAY GET OUT OF TOWN,
BUT YOU'RE STARTING,
BEGINNING,
BECOMING A CLOWN

BEFORE THE NOSE, THE WIG, THE SHOES,
BEFORE YOU PAY YOUR CLOWNY DUES
IT STARTS WITH ONE JOKE, BUT THEN IT GREW

BECAUSE YOU'RE STARTING,
BEGINNING,
BECOMING,

STARTING,
BEGINNING,
BECOMING A CLOWN

FUNNY AIN'T EASY,
BUT CLOWNIN' AIN'T HARD
TEN CLOWNS BURIED
IN MY BACK YARD
IT STARTED SO PURE,
BUT IT GOT MARRED

AND NOW YOU KNOW
I TRIED TO TELL YOU SO,
TELL YOU SO

BUT YOU COULDN'T HEAR ME
OVER YOUR SQUEAKY SHOES
DIDN'T WANT TO BE NEAR ME,
HANG 'ROUND MY CIRCUS BLUES

NO NEED TO FEAR ME
'CAUSE I'M A CLOWN LIKE YOU

AND YOU'RE

STARTING,
BEGINNING,
BECOMING,

STARTING,
BEGINNING,
BECOMING,

STARTING,
BEGINNING,
BECOMING
A CLOWN
A CLOWN
A CLOOOOOOOOOOWN

> (**MAC** *should be full-clown by now. If not, maybe sing "a clown" a few more times until he's ready.*)

> (**GLORIA** *puts in an earpiece.*)

MAC. Can you hear me?

GLORIA. Loud and clear.

MAC. So I guess, yeah, really doing this undercover-clown thing.

GLORIA. You think it was Brigham Bill's boys that done it?

MAC. Could be. They're the only other big-time clown cartel.

GLORIA. There's some small-time players.

MAC. Sure. The small-time maybe want a place in the big show. Or it's an inside job.

GLORIA. We'll find out soon enough if you blend in good enough.

MAC. Oh, I blend.

GLORIA. Yeah, you blend. Look, Mac, I wanted to say...

MAC. Is it about being careful?

GLORIA. Yeah but no.

MAC. Is it about carrying multiple guns?

GLORIA. Yeah but no.

MAC. Is it about thinking on my feet?

GLORIA. Yeah but no.

MAC. Is it – is it about us?

GLORIA. Uhhhhsssssssssssssssssssssssss? No. No. No. No. No. No.

MAC. Oh.

GLORIA. No. Let's just do the job.

MAC. Yeah.

GLORIA. You're a good cop.

MAC. Thanks.

GLORIA. And Mac?

MAC. Yeah.

GLORIA. Don't forget to be funny.

> *(Lights change.* **MAC** *is behind the bar.* **MUSTY** *and* **PETUNIA** *watch him.* **POPO** *enters.)*

POPO. *(About clown* **MAC.***)* You want me to hire him as a bartender? And you vouch for him?

PETUNIA. Yeah, I vouch for him. He's a good guy.

MUSTY. A good fella?

PETUNIA. You'll like him.

POPO. Don't tell me what I like!

PETUNIA. Sorry. Sorry, Popo.

POPO. I like sushi.

PETUNIA. Sorry.

POPO. I like knives.

PETUNIA. Sorry.

POPO. I like school supplies.

PETUNIA. Sorry. Sorry. Sorry.

POPO. I like cashmere. I like to hear their last words right before they die. I like type-A blood. I like sunsets. I like a sock with an orange in it. I like a roll of quarters. I like laughing. I like hobo clowns. I like divorce when it's the right decision. I like bodies of water. I like hippos. I like getting paid on time. I like ice picks. I like swordfish. I like love letters. I like killing. I like to kill. I like making people die. Killing. Killed. Killered. Killingly. Killperson. Kill-kill-kill-kill-kkkkkk. Dead. That's what I like. Don't tell me what I like!

PETUNIA. Sorry Popo.

POPO. What's your name, kid?

MAC. Nickels.

POPO. No. We already got a Nickels. We could call you Pickles.

MAC. Uh, okay. It's just that I don't like pickles. Or cucumbers.

POPO. Pickles, are you bein' fussy?

MAC. No. No. I wasn't.

PETUNIA. Yeah, don't. She hates fussy.

POPO. I hate fussy. Musty, test him on the drinks.

(**MUSTY** *comes to the bar.*)

MUSTY. What can you make, kid?

MAC. What'll you have?

[MUSIC NO. 03 "BARTENDER SONG"]

MUSTY.
MAKE ME A MANHATTAN,

A COSMO AND MARTINI
A MOJITO, A COSMO AND A BELLINI
A SIDECAR, A STINGER,
A MAI-TAI, AND BRING HER
A BLACK RUSSIAN, A COSMO AND FLIRTINI

> (**MAC** *makes these very fast, instantaneously, much faster than anyone could make these.* **POPO** *drinks them.*)

POPO. What else?

MAC.

I CAN MAKE GIN TONIC, GIN ROCKS, AND GIN RUMMY

POPO. Can you make it funny?

MAC.

A MANHATTAN LIGHT A FIRE IN YOUR TUMMY

POPO. Can you make it funny?

MAC.

VODKA WITH THREE TYPES OF GUMMIES.

POPO. But but but but can you make it funny?

> (*A lazzo in which* **MAC** *makes it funny. Spraying seltzer? Honking a horn over it? Blowing bubbles in it? Putting a clown nose on the rim? Putting small clown feet in front of it? Something that's trying very hard. In any case, he has made it funny. Song ends.*)

Okay. You're hired.

> (*Exit* **POPO.**)

MAC. I made it funny, right? She didn't laugh.

MUSTY. It wasn't that funny, kid.

MAC. Yeah but –

MUSTY. Drop it.

>(**MAC** *maybe literally drops something he was holding.*)

(Can say "tisk," or make another disapproving noise.)
Tsk.

MAC. So, uh, real shame about Happy, huh?

MUSTY. I guess.

MAC. But maybe some people were mad at him.

MUSTY. Everybody's mad at everybody.

MAC. Yeah but who was mad at Happy? What happened to him exactly? Do you know? You can tell me.

MUSTY. Shut up, kid. The ladies is coming.

>(**PETUNIA** *gets on the stage and does a burlesque show.* **HOHO, JELLY B,** *and* **VIRGINIA** *enter and dance provocatively in different spaces.*)

MAC. Wow.

>(**VIRGINIA** *is closest to* **MAC.** *He is transfixed by her. When* **PETUNIA**'s *act comes to an end, they talk. It should be very clear that* **MAC** *is into her and is having new feelings.*)

VIRGINIA. Fresh meat! What's your name?

MAC. Ma– I mean Nick– I mean Pickles, ma'am.

VIRGINIA. Ain't no ma'am here. I'm Virginia. But my friends call me Ginny. Or Virginny. Or Vir-gin-gin. *(Provocatively.)* Or Vah Juh Juh.

MAC. Vah –

VIRGINIA. You're so cute. Where have you been hiding?

MAC. Nowhere, ma'a– uh Virginia.

VIRGINIA. In Virginia! That's my name, you know.

MAC. No. I know. I wasn't saying I was in Virginia.

VIRGINIA. I feel like I would know if you were. A big boy like you.

MAC. Ha Ha! Heh. Ha! You're kind of a lot.

VIRGINIA. In a good way, though, right?

MAC. Heh. Yeah.

VIRGINIA. You have no idea how good. Don't go nowhere, cutie.

MAC. Oh! Ha! Where would I go.

VIRGINIA. I like you. You're funny.

(**VIRGINIA** *exits to work the room.*)

MAC. She thinks I'm funny.

(**CLITEAU, CLITEAU** *enters. He is a mime. He gets on the stage and does an elaborate mime act. He has a French accent. When he describes his miming actions, he tells us what he's doing in an exaggerated shout.*)

Who's that?

MUSTY. That's Cliteau, Cliteau. He thinks he's fancy 'cause he studied in Paris. I shit on Paris.

CLITEAU, CLITEAU. Shut up! (*Shouting.*) I'm pulling a rope now!

MUSTY. I shit on Paris' shitty filthy streets.

CLITEAU, CLITEAU. Shut up!

MUSTY. I shit on the Louvre! I shit on the Mona Lisa and the Van Goghs and all the impressionists! Maybe not on Monet.

CLITEAU, CLITEAU. I'm making art up here and you're interrupting!

MUSTY. That's not art.

CLITEAU, CLITEAU. I'm trapped inside a box now!

MUSTY. Your box sucks! I shit on your box!

CLITEAU, CLITEAU. How will I get out?! How will I get out? I'm out. Now I'm climbing a ladder. Look at me!

MUSTY. Ladders aren't even like that. That's a terrible ladder!

CLITEAU, CLITEAU. Now I'm on the high wire. This is some fucking art. You can almost see it can't you? I learned this shit in Paris.

MUSTY. Fucking idiot. Watch this. He always gets eaten by a bear at the end.

MAC. Are you kidding?

MUSTY. No. He thinks it's dramatic or beautiful or some shit. Wait for it. Wait for it. Fucking idiot.

CLITEAU, CLITEAU. Ahhhh! It's got me. It's got my leg. No! I didn't see your cubs. Please! Ahhhh! Ahhhh! Argh! Where's my bear spray?!

(**CLITEAU, CLITEAU** *takes a long time to die.*)

MUSTY. I hate him.

(*Exit* **MUSTY.** **VIRGINIA** *approaches the bar.*)

VIRGINIA. I need a Suck, Bang and a Blow, Sex on My Face, Slow Comfortable Screw Against the Wall, Royal Fuck, Tight Snatch and a Screaming Orgasm.

MAC. (*Titillated and uncomfortable.*) Uh. Okay!

CLITEAU, CLITEAU. Uugh.

VIRGINIA. Oh and make 'em funny.

> (**MAC** *quickly makes a series of drinks for* **VIRGINIA**. *While he is doing this,* **BILLY BILL** *and* **WILLIAMY BILL** *enter. They are cowboy mobster clowns. They drawl.* **CLITEAU, CLITEAU** *continues to die onstage.*)

BILLY BILL. Sheeyucks! *(He's saying shucks.)* Where's Happy at?

PETUNIA. Billy Bill. And Williamy Bill.

CLITEAU, CLITEAU. Uugh.

MUSTY. What are Brigham Bill's boys doing in here?

CLITEAU, CLITEAU. The bear's got me! Aaah!

PETUNIA. What are you doing here, Billy Bill? And Williamy Bill too?

BILLY BILL. Shoot! I don't answer questions. I ask questions. And my question is thus: Where's Happy at? I need to conversate with him.

CLITEAU, CLITEAU. It hurts so much! I won't live much longer. Aaagh the pain.

BILLY BILL. Shut him up.

> (**WILLIAMY BILL** *shoots* **CLITEAU, CLITEAU** *dead. He dies very quickly.*)

MUSTY. What'ja do that for?

BILLY BILL. You didn't like him.

MUSTY. I know, but –

WILLIAMY BILL. Now you get more stage time.

MUSTY. I know but. You killed our only mime.

PETUNIA. We don't got another.

WILLIAMY BILL. You'll get another.

PETUNIA. I mean, he's right. We could get another. Maybe a mimier mime.

VIRGINIA. I kinda liked that one. Or maybe I didn't *like* him. I didn't mind him. Yeah. I didn't mind the mime. He was fine.

MAC. I think I'm in shock.

BILLY BILL. Where's Happy at?

POPO. *(Entering.)* He's not here. Why don't you and Williamy Bill come to the back room and we'll have a conversation. Leave your gats here.

PETUNIA. I ken hold 'em.

BILLY BILL. Shoot! We don't got to do that.

POPO. I could end the conversation now if you know what I mean.

MAC. I think I know what she means.

PETUNIA. She means she's going to kill them. Probably with a slash to the jugular. Before they can even reach for they piece. She can do them both at the same time. She's like a ninja but funny.

BILLY BILL. All right. All right. Hold yer horses.

>(**BILLY BILL** *and* **WILLIAMY BILL** *put their guns on the bar. There are a lot of guns. It takes a while. This is another lazzi punctuated by music.* **PETUNIA** *takes them away in several trips offstage. When they are done –)*

POPO. And now pay for the mess you made.

WILLIAMY BILL. What mess?

POPO. The bloody mime on the stage. Got to be cleaned up and also the cost of makin' the body disappear. And pay for the time it'll take me to interview a new mime. And a fee for your ugly face. And an asshole tax.

And also pay for the drink I'm going to drink after our meeting.

> (**BILLY BILL** *throws some money on the floor.* **PETUNIA** *picks it up.* **POPO** *leads* **BILLY BILL** *and* **WILLIAMY BILL** *offstage.)*

MAC. *(Shaky.)* Wow. That's the first dead clown I ever seen.

VIRGINIA. It's a mime.

MAC. I wonder what's happening in that office.

MUSTY. Stop wondering things, kid. Keep out of other people's business. It's one of the rules. You know the rules?

MAC. Yeah. Course I know the rules.

MUSTY. You gotta know the rules. You want me to teach you the rules?

VIRGINIA. I'll teach him the rules.

MAC. I know the rules.

MUSTY. Stop asking questions then.

MAC. Yeah, of course. It's just – Where is Happy? And is Popo in charge now? Did Popo kill Happy? Did Brigham Bill's boys do it and pretend like they didn't know he was dead when they came in? Is this a hostile takeover? Or did they come to buy the bar? If I'm not careful with my mouth, are you gonna know I'm out of my element here and also not that experienced with ladies?

MUSTY. I really thought I said stop asking questions.

VIRGINIA. Leave him alone. He's not used to the violence. I'll take care of him. When I'm done with him, he'll be right as rain. But like a sexy rain. Like busting a nut but a beautiful busting, you know? The French call it a little death. Poetical. Like rain.

MUSTY. Whatever. I hate the French. Except Monet.

(*Exit* MUSTY.)

VIRGINIA. You want to see a show, kid? Like a real show? None of this kid stuff.

MAC. What?

VIRGINIA. Just sit back, relax. Have a drink. I'll do my show.

MAC. I don't know.

VIRGINIA. What don't you know?

MAC. I don't know what I don't know.

VIRGINIA. Whatsamatter? You never been with a clown before?

MAC. Course I have. Course. Just give me a minute to compose myself.

VIRGINIA. Sure. I got to get ready anyway.

(MAC *is now on the stage alone.*)

MAC. (*Talking into his wire.*) Gloria, this isn't working. I didn't get a chance to bug the office. I'm not fitting in. I need some backup here. I saw a murder. We could take Williamy Bill out in cuffs now or wait and see. I don't know. I don't think I can do this alone anymore. And also Virginia is going to come back and do some kind of sexual dance and I think there are expectations and yeah I mean she's attractive. The clown life is attractive. I see that now. I mean maybe less killing but overall, I'm feeling kind of tingly and in over my head and I think I should maybe go now...unless –

(*Enter* VIRGINIA.)

VIRGINIA. You talking to somebody?

MAC. You.

VIRGINIA. Hold onto your socks. You never seen nothing like this.

> (**VIRGINIA** *begins to do a burlesque just for* **MAC.** *As* **MAC** *becomes deeply uncomfortable,* **GLORIA** *arrives, dressed as a clown. She also does a burlesque that competes directly with* **VIRGINIA.**)

GLORIA. Oh yeah?! Check me out!

MAC. Gloria? I mean, "Who is this mysterious clown?"

> (**PETUNIA** *watches and may provide commentary: "Whoa! Lookit that! New girl brought her A-game!" etc. When the song has ended, if they are shoving each other or something, or* **VIRGINIA** *pulls a knife maybe,* **PETUNIA** *breaks it up.*)

PETUNIA. Hey hey. She won fair and square.

VIRGINIA. That was my time. The new girl's gotta learn. Who are you?

GLORIA. They call me Snapsy.

VIRGINIA. More like Snatchy. Get your hands off my man.

PETUNIA. Not now. On your own time. Get back to work Virginia. Snapsy, with me.

> (**VIRGINIA** *exits.*)

GLORIA. I felt like he needed some backup.

PETUNIA. Sure. We all need backup. But we don't all always get it. I wish I had backup. No one ever backs me up. Not since Happy.

MAC. You didn't have to do that.

GLORIA. You told me to come.

MAC. I know. I'm glad you're here. I mean the other thing. The dancing.

GLORIA. You didn't like it?

MAC. I didn't say that.

GLORIA. What are you saying?

MAC. Nothing. I'm not saying anything.

GLORIA. Me either.

MAC. Me either.

GLORIA. But if you were saying something –

MAC. But I'm not. Are you?

GLORIA. No.

MAC. Okay.

GLORIA. Okay.

MAC. You look good as a clown.

GLORIA. So do you.

MAC. Not that you don't look good normally.

GLORIA. Yeah. You too.

MAC. Are we in love with each other?

GLORIA. Yes.

MAC. We should get back to work though, right?

GLORIA. Right. *(To* **PETUNIA**, *who has been standing there the whole time.)* Is there another way in that back office?

PETUNIA. We could throw a flash grenade in there. Or release some mice. We could drill a hole in the wall. Or listen at the door with a glass. We could lure Williamy Bill out with a honey pot. He likes the lady clowns. Especially the seltzer sluts. Or we could blow up the bar.

GLORIA. No.

PETUNIA. I was just spitballin'.

MAC. I just wish it was bugged.

PETUNIA. Why don't we just tell 'em it is?

GLORIA. Genius!

PETUNIA. *(Running toward the office.)* Popo! Get outta there right now! The office is bugged.

(Enter **POPO,** *followed by* **BILLY BILL** *and* **WILLIAMY BILL.***)*

POPO. How do you know?

PETUNIA. Uh! Twinkles just called and told me.

POPO. I didn't hear the phone ring.

PETUNIA. He called my cell. I have it on vibrate. Sometimes I just let it ring and ring. And ring.

BILLY BILL. Do we trust Twinkles?

WILLIAMY BILL. I don't trust Twinkles as fer as I ken throw him.

POPO. I don't trust you. We can talk out here.

BILLY BILL. Do we trust them?

WILLIAMY BILL. I don't trust them as fer as I ken throw 'em.

POPO. They understand what happens if they cross Popo.

MUSTY. No one crosses Popo.

POPO. You! Sing us a song. You! Get us a drink.

BILLY BILL. What about our business conversing?

POPO. After the song.

MAC. Whattaya want?

POPO. Gimme a Clownface Slobber. Heavy on the rye and funny as cancer.

BILLY BILL. Bartender's Crowbar with three umbrellas. No rocks. Dead steer.

WILLIAMY BILL. Sex in the Funny Papers. Hold the onion. Hold the presses. Extra pancetta. With a tadpole. Salted, not stirred. No pickle. Sprinkled under a cherry moon. But no day passes. King Tut it, flip it, and ice it, but light it up. Drop the barrel in the bushes but leave the staves all quiet on the western front. Wave the red cape in front of it. Run it by the doughboy, feed it bread and honey, give it to the fisherman's daughter and stick its head in the oven.

MAC. Fruit?

WILLIAMY BILL. *(No.)* Scurvy.

(**MAC** *makes these drinks quickly.*)

BILLY BILL. Can we converse now?

POPO. You can talk but I think we're at a standstill.

BILLY BILL. Where's Happy at? He was the one we was supposed to do the deal with.

POPO. You're asking me where Happy is?

WILLIAMY BILL. Yup. Where's Happy at?

POPO. You ask me that again, I'm going to take my knife and stick it though your eye socket and lobotomize you.

WILLIAMY BILL. What'd I say?

POPO. You're saying you don't know what happened to Happy?

BILLY BILL. What happened to Happy?

POPO. Look I don't want to talk to you. I only want to talk to Brigham Bill. Call him right now and get him over here.

BILLY BILL. Sheeyuks! Brigham Bill don't want me to do that.

POPO. Call him or I send you out in pieces.

*(***BILLY BILL*** *sighs. Makes a call.)*

BILLY BILL. Yeah. Happy ain't here. Popo says she only deal with you. Yeah. The Macarena. Yeah. *All About Eve.* Yeah. Dylan Thomas. No, not Danny Thomas. No. You're thinking of Dave Thomas the founder of Wendy's. Yeah. Origami. Sweater vest. Octopuses. No, Octopi is wrong. It's octopuses. Blood oranges. *The Quick and the Dead.* Bananas. I had to fire that monkey. I had to. I had to. Okay. *(Hangs up.)* He's not happy there's no Happy but he's coming.

POPO. *(To* **MUSTY.***)* Didn't I say sing?

MUSTY. This song is dedicated to Brigham Bill's Boys. Hi Boys. Brigham Bill's Circus is almost like a real circus if it was created by someone who has no idea what a circus is. Like Brigham read *Family Circus* and was like I can do this and then he hired a bunch of monkeys.

POPO. Just sing the song.

[MUSIC NO. 04 "NEVER TRUST A CLOWN"]

MUSTY.
> DON'T NEVER TRUST NOBODY,
> BUT NEVER TRUST A CLOWN
> YOU THINK YOU HAVE A BUDDY
> HE'LL RUN YOUR SHIP AGROUND
>
> CLOWNS WILL STAB YOU IN THE BACK
> CLOWNS WILL EAT YOUR LUNCH
> CLOWNS KIDNAP YOUR MOTHER
> AND TAKE HER OUT TO BRUNCH
>
> CLOWNS CAN KILL
> CLOWNS CAN MAIM
> CLOWNS ARE PSYCHO CRAY CRAY INSANE

CLOWNS ARE STABBY
CLOWNS PLAY GAMES
CLOWNS ARE OUTSIDE IN THE RAIN

CLOWNS WILL KICK YOU DOWN THE STREET
CLOWNS WILL MAKE YOU CRY
IF YOU THINK YOU FOUND A CLOWN TO LOVE,
CLOWNS MIGHT MAKE YOU DIE

ALL THE CLOWNS I EVER KNEW
AND ALL THE CLOWNS I KNOW
CAME TOGETHER ONE DAY IN ONE PLACE
AND THERE WAS SUCH A ROW

CLOWNS OF ALL SHAPES AND SIZE,
CLOWNS WHO KILL AND EXERCISE
CLOWNS WILL CUT YOU INTO FRIES
NEVER TRUST A CLOWN

There's a saying my mother taught me.

It goes like this.

"Keep your hands where I can see 'em

and don't believe anything said out the side of my mouth."

You couldn't trust my mother, though.

She was a clown too.

DON'T NEVER TRUST NOBODY
BUT NEVER TRUST A CLOWN
YOU THINK YOU HAVE A BUDDY
HE'LL RUN YOUR SHIP AGROUND

Reminds me of a joke. Brigham Bill's Circus is so bad.

ALL. How bad is it?

MUSTY. They can't afford a bear so it's just a bunch of monkeys in a bear costume.

(Cymbal punctuation for punchline.)

MUSTY. Thank you. Thank you. No, but really. Brigham Bill's Circus is so bad.

ALL. How bad is it?

MUSTY. The lion tamer got eaten by a housecat.

(Cymbal punctuation for punchline.)

No but seriously. It's a really terrible circus. Are you curious how terrible?

ALL. Yes.

MUSTY. I don't want to say they're dirty but the acrobats gave the high wire syphilis.

> *(**WILLIAMY BILL** and **BILLY BILL** are getting upset. Maybe they make to rush the stage and they are stopped.)*

POPO. Just sing the song, Musty.

MUSTY.

CLOWNS CAN KILL
CLOWNS CAN MAIM
CLOWNS ARE PSYCHO CRAY CRAY INSANE
CLOWNS ARE STABBY
CLOWNS PLAY GAMES
CLOWNS ARE OUTSIDE IN THE RAIN

NEVER TRUST,
NEVER TRUST,
NEVER TRUST A CLOWN
NEVER TRUST,
NEVER TRUST,
NEVER TRUST A CLOWN
NEVER TRUST,
NEVER TRUST,
NEVER TRUST A CLOWN

NEVER TRUST,
NEVER TRUST A CLOWN!!!!!

> *(After applause has died down,* **BRIGHAM**
> **BILL** *enters. He wears a cowboy hat and has*
> *an exaggerated drawl.)*

PETUNIA. Brigham!

BRIGHAM BILL. Well howdy do, Clown Bar. Brigham Bill has arrived. I is he. What got you all tied up like yesterday's steer?

POPO. Put the gun on the table. Then we can talk.

BRIGHAM BILL. Brigham Bill don't surrender no gun for nobody.

POPO. I'm not nobody. I'm Popo.

MAC. I'm nobody. Not that anyone should pay attention to me at all. Look away. I'm just a bartender. Nothing more.

POPO. Shut up, kid.

BRIGHAM BILL. I expect I can't have the meeting I was expecting to have. Where's Happy at?

POPO. Put the gun on the table, Brigham. I'm a faster draw than you.

BRIGHAM BILL. Then whatchu worried about, Lil' Popo?

POPO. Gun on the table. I'm not gonna say it again. Don't test me.

BRIGHAM BILL. Why is it when someone say, "Don't test me," I want to test 'em? Maybe it's the cowboy in me.

POPO. You're from Jersey.

WILLIAMY BILL. West Jersey.

> **(POPO** *shoots* **WILLIAMY BILL,** *who dies.*
> **BRIGHAM BILL** *draws, and* **POPO** *shoots the*
> *gun out of his hand.)*

BRIGHAM BILL. What are you going and getting violent fer? I thought we were having a meeting. That was my fifth-favorite relative you just killed off.

POPO. He's annoying.

BRIGHAM BILL. I know'd it. But still. What the fuck, Popo?

POPO. You shouldn't have kilt Happy.

BRIGHAM BILL. Me? I didn't do that.

POPO. I don't believe you.

BRIGHAM BILL. I'm serious as a scorpion. We was making a deal.

PETUNIA. What kind of deal?

BRIGHAM BILL. We was supposed to buy him out. He said to me, "Listen Bill."

(**HAPPY** *appears in a memory.*)

HAPPY. Listen Bill. I want to get out of the game. You want my territory?

BRIGHAM BILL. You know I do.

HAPPY. You want the business?

BRIGHAM BILL. Heck yes, Happy.

HAPPY. If you got the cash, we can make a deal.

BRIGHAM BILL. Yee haw! That's what I like. But where will you go? Back to the force?

HAPPY. Don't worry about me. I'll be fine. You just get your ducks in a row.

(*Exit* **HAPPY.**)

BRIGHAM BILL. And my ducks is all lined up like in a line, like on a fence. But Happy ain't here.

POPO. Because you killed him.

BRIGHAM BILL. Why would I do that?

POPO. Hostile takeover.

BRIGHAM BILL. That's not my style.

MUSTY. He's right. Brigham Bill is so bad at organized crime.

ALL. How bad is he?

MUSTY. It's not a joke. He's just really bad at it. They don't make much money. Their prostitutes have rough hands. Their drugs are mostly rat poison. Um. Their hired killers are always getting popped. But most of all, they just don't really inspire confidence, you know? Like if I go into business with them, will I even get paid? If I have to go rough someone up, are they going to send a chimpanzee to help me? And can I trust the chimp when the shit goes down? I mean I know some of them are well trained but at the end of the day, they're really just dumb animals, not unlike the humans who also work with Brigham Bill. They're so stupid.

ALL. How stupid are they?

BRIGHAM BILL. I take exception.

MUSTY. With what part?

BRIGHAM BILL. Our chimps are the best pickpockets in town.

MUSTY. Okay but then how do you prevent them from eating the money?

BRIGHAM BILL. You gots to take it out of theya hands. But they can't rat you out and they can't go to jail. 'Cause, you know. They're chimps.

GLORIA. You're saying your whiz mob is mostly trained monkeys?

BRIGHAM BILL. Chimpanzees are not monkeys! They're chimpanzees! They are apes. They don't have tails. Monkeys have tails. Chimps don't have tails.

MAC. Do they have a little bit of fluff like a rabbit?

BRIGHAM BILL. Do you have a little bit of fluff?! Because chimps and people are closely related.

GLORIA. Okay. Let's forget about the tails.

POPO. Who is you?

GLORIA. What? I'm Snapsy.

POPO. We already have a Snapsy. You can be Dripsy.

GLORIA. Um. Do I have to be?

POPO. Yes. But the trouble is, I've seen you before. Petunia, do I know her?

PETUNIA. I don't think so.

POPO. You're a clown, huh?

GLORIA. Yeah.

POPO. You work the big show?

GLORIA. I worked the Big Cherry Circus in DC.

POPO. Yeah, I know it. What's your specialty? Juggling? Seal training? Bear wrestling? Unicycle? Spit take? Cats? Pie eating? Pool leaping? Frog racing? Acrobatics? Porn? Synchronized skating? Baking? Mice? Palm reading? Barista?

GLORIA. Knife throwing.

POPO. I'd like to see that sometime.

GLORIA. Sure.

POPO. I really would.

GLORIA. Any time.

> (*Silence as* **POPO** *looks at* **GLORIA** *for a long time.*)

POPO. (*Pointing at* **GLORIA**.) Cop! She's a cop!

PETUNIA. Uh.

> (GLORIA *ducks. Everyone starts shooting, including* BILLY BILL, *who had one more gun he never gave up.* MAC *is trying to provide cover.*)

BRIGHAM BILL. Cops! Not cops! I hate cops!

GLORIA. Stop! Popo! We're on the same side.

POPO. I ain't on the side a no cop!

PETUNIA. Hold on a sec.

MAC. You don't understand!

POPO. The bartender too! That was my third-favorite bartender.

> (*Everyone is shooting and ducking and rolling.*)

MUSTY. Not as good as Thumbs.

POPO. Thumbs was really good.

MUSTY. It was the extra olives. Thumbs always put in extra olives.

MAC. You could have told me. I could have put in extra olives.

MUSTY. Yeah but Thumbs just knew. You never had to ask.

PETUNIA. Stop! Stop! Stop! Stop shooting! Stop it!

> (PETUNIA *blows an air horn or loud whistle. Everyone stops shooting.*)

I told them to come.

POPO. You did what?

PETUNIA. I invited the cops here. To find out who killed Happy.

POPO. I see. But the thing is, you lie down with cops, you stand up covered in cops. Filthy animals. I need to take a shower.

BRIGHAM BILL. I hate cops!

PETUNIA. I know but they're here to help.

POPO. Petunia, sometimes I think –

MUSTY. Watch out!

(**BILLY BILL** *has come up behind* **POPO***, aims his gun at her.*)

(**GLORIA** *throws a knife – actually she makes a throwing motion, and* **BILLY BILL** *holds a knife to his chest like she just threw it at him. He falls. He dies, quickly.*)

BILLY BILL. Ugh!

POPO. You just save me, copper?

GLORIA. I might've.

BRIGHAM BILL. That was my third-favorite son!

POPO. He was as dumb as bricks.

BRIGHAM BILL. I knowed it. But some of them bricks was my DNA. And I ain't gonna stand fer it! Also now I'm going to kill you all and take over this business. Hostile takeover motherfuckers! Yippee Kiii Yay!

(**BRIGHAM BILL** *starts shooting at everyone, and everyone starts shooting at him.*)

POPO. Bill, you're not getting out of here alive.

BRIGHAM BILL. I might!

PETUNIA. You won't!

BRIGHAM BILL. I could!

POPO. Nope.

BRIGHAM BILL. Winner takes all and sometimes, once in a while, upon a lone blue prairie moon, Brigham Bill catches a break and Brigham Bill wins.

(**MUSTY** *takes a stray bullet.*)

MUSTY. AARH!

PETUNIA. You shot Musty!

MUSTY. It's okay. It's just my arm.

(**MUSTY** *gets shot again.*)

And my leg! (*Shot again.*) And my other leg! (*Shot again.*) And my chest. (*Shot again.*) And my head.

(*While* **BRIGHAM BILL** *has been shooting* **MUSTY**, **POPO** *has snuck up on him, maybe climbing under a table or vaulting a table or somersaulting or something. She grabs* **BRIGHAM BILL** *and slits his throat. He falls dead.*)

(*Weakly.*) I knew Brigham Bill was never going to take over. He's not good.

ALL. How bad is he?

MUSTY. (*Weakly.*) Don't do that now. There is something I should maybe say. I have useful information maybe. I mean I did see Happy get killed. So there's that. I was in the room. No one ever notices the singer, do they? Not really. Not when the singer is me anyway. You see, a few days ago, Twinkles came in to talk to Happy.

ALL. Twinkles!

MUSTY.

TWINKLE TWINKLE LITTLE CLOWN.

(*Coughs and coughs.*)

(**HAPPY** *is at a table.* **TWINKLES** *approaches.*)

HAPPY. Twinkles, my oldest friend. What can I do for you?

TWINKLES. I hear you're selling out to Brigham Bill.

HAPPY. Brigham Bill has a big mouth.

TWINKLES. You know he'll run this bar into the ground.

HAPPY. He can't do worse than me. Twink, I'm a terrible mob boss. I got to get out. You should do the same, before it's too late. Go to the feds, tell them what you know. They'll give you a better life.

TWINKLES. Maybe you could do that.

HAPPY. I can't. I'm the top of the chain. I'll be ratting myself out.

TWINKLES. You can't sell the Clown Bar. Not to Brigham Bill. Not to anyone. It's the most special place that's ever existed and I'd rather die than let the Clown Bar die.

HAPPY. It's not up to you.

TWINKLES. I could put two in your head right now.

HAPPY. You'd do me like that Twinkles?

TWINKLES. Leave the bar to me. Run off, take the paint off your face. Start your life over. Maybe take Petunia with you. You could do worse.

HAPPY. I don't love her.

TWINKLES. There's always Clown Island. You think it exists?

HAPPY. I don't know if it does or it doesn't. The streets they say are paved with glitter. Everyone's your friend and everyone's a clown. No crime, not even clown crime. What's mine is yours and what's yours is at the bottom of this pie tin.

TWINKLES. They say it's a very funny paradise.

HAPPY. But the boats don't go there. You have to know someone who knows someone who has a helicopter and knows the route. You have to be lucky. I was never lucky. And anyway, you know it doesn't really exist. Not really. It's just a story to tell little clowns.

TWINKLES. So you'll let the Clown Bar go down then?

HAPPY. What do you want me to do? I made some mistakes. I got sloppy. The fuzz is closing in. It was never a sustainable life, the clown crime life.

TWINKLES. I'm not letting you do this.

HAPPY. Well I'm not changing my mind, so you'll have to shoot me.

TWINKLES. I've shot clowns before.

HAPPY. Then shoot me, Twinkles. Empty out the safe, Turn state's evidence. And when you come back years later, wearing a disguise, maybe just maybe the Clown Bar will still be here. But if you're not prepared to shoot me, you better walk out right now. Because I'm selling and there ain't nothing you can –

(**TWINKLES** *shoots him in the head.*)

TWINKLES. I'm sorry.

(**TWINKLES** *removes* **HAPPY**'s *clown nose. Puts it on the desk.*)

I loved you, you bastard.

(*Exit* **TWINKLES**. *End of memory.*)

MUSTY.
TWINKLES TWINKLES, LITTLE BITCH,
HAPPY KILLER AND A SNITCH

(**MUSTY** *dies.* **POPO** *pulls him offstage.*)

MAC. Clowns keep dying.

PETUNIA. It's the life.

MAC. So really that entire time he was just in the corner and neither of them saw him?

GLORIA. I'm sorry, Petunia.

PETUNIA. I knowed he was dead. I just didn't think...

MAC. Like he was just sitting there?

POPO. We're gonna need another singer.

PETUNIA. I'll take care of it.

POPO. You coppers still moving in? You gonna shut us down?

MAC. All our intel was Happy-specific. We got nothin'.

POPO. So Twinkles is useless anyway.

GLORIA. Kinda. Yeah.

POPO. But he still gets away.

PETUNIA. I don't like that.

MAC. I don't like it much either.

POPO. You still wearing a wire?

(**MAC** *makes a show of unplugging his wire.*)

Good. Good. Well, it seems like you know the whereabouts of the safe house where Twinkles is being held. Maybe you could draw a map and accidentally leave it where someone could see it.

MAC. He did it for you.

POPO. I didn't ask him to. Petunia you ask Twinkles to kill Happy to save the bar?

PETUNIA. No.

POPO. Then it's settled.

MAC. Let me sidebar with my partner.

PETUNIA. I want to talk to you anyway, Popo.

> *(MAC and GLORIA whisper to each other.)*

I know you was just taking care of the bar until Happy came back. You didn't really have designs on bein' the boss did you?

POPO. Not really.

PETUNIA. 'Cause I was thinking. There's a lot of accounting and organizing involved with bossing. Payroll. Money laundering. Lots of phone calls and cooking the books. And scheduling people, calling in hits. Lots of administration.

POPO. I'm a killer. I ain't no administrator.

PETUNIA. You're the most terrifying killer that every existed.

POPO. Yeah.

PETUNIA. So let me run the business. I'm a lot smarter than everyone thinks. I already know how everything runs.

POPO. Okay.

PETUNIA. Okay? But will you work for me.

POPO. Okay.

PETUNIA. And have my back?

POPO. I promise.

PETUNIA. Then maybe, just maybe we can keep it all up and running.

POPO. Our competition is gone.

PETUNIA. That it is. You did real good, Popo. Oh and one more thing. I want to do the hit.

POPO. Yeah?

PETUNIA. Yeah. It's personal.

> *(MAC and GLORIA come out of their huddle.)*

GLORIA. Okay.

MAC. We talked it over.

> (*He unrolls a map they just drew.* **PETUNIA** *takes it and exits.*)
>
> (*A clown –* **GUSTY** *– who looks exactly like* **MUSTY** *goes over to the mic and clears his throat.*)

GUSTY. Ahem. Anyone want to hear a song?

GLORIA. Who's that?

POPO. Oh that's Gusty – Dusty and Musty's cousin.

GUSTY. I said does anyone want to hear a song?

> (**POPO** *exits to the back.* **MAC** *approaches* **GUSTY**.)

MAC. I got a request. (*Whispers to* **GUSTY**.)

GUSTY. Really? I don't think that's what the room wants right now.

MAC. Please sing the song.

GUSTY. Let me take a break first.

MAC. You just got here.

GUSTY. What the fuck do you know about it. Where's the bartender?

MAC. I'll make it. What do you want?

GUSTY. Gimme a salty trombone. Heavy on the absinthe. A little light in the loafers.

> (**MAC** *makes him a drink.* **GLORIA** *approaches.*)

GLORIA. I guess we should go then.

MAC. Yeah.

GLORIA. It's not our world, Mac.

MAC. I know, but…

GLORIA. The clown ladies?

MAC. No. No. I mean, I like how you look.

GLORIA. Yeah.

MAC. And I like how I feel too. When I'm dressed like this.

GLORIA. And you're pretty funny.

MAC. I am, aren't I? I really liked making drinks.

GLORIA. Make me one, will you?

MAC. What do you want?

GLORIA. Surprise me.

>   (**MAC** *makes her a drink.*)

You know, we don't have to take the makeup off yet.

MAC. But we're not clowns are we?

GLORIA. You know what they say? Once a clown, always a clown.

> *(A choreographed dance of sorts.* **GLORIA** *and* **MAC** *start making out as* **GUSTY** *sings "Clown Love." It gets hot and heavy and heavier. Maybe they go offstage or have some onstage, mostly-clothed sex in a booth or in shadow behind a screen.)*

[MUSIC NO. 05 "CLOWN LOVE"]

GUSTY.
YOUR NOSE – IS THE BEST CLOWN NOSE I HAVE EVER
    KNOWN. MM
YOUR TOES – ARE THE BEST CLOWN TOES THAT I HAVE
    EVER KNOWN
YOUR EYES – SPARKLE IN THE NIGHT

LIKE A NIGHT – THIS ONE NIGHT – WHERE EV'RYTHING
    SPARKLES THAT NIGHT
CLOWN LOVE! IT'S LOVE BETWEEN A CLOWN AND A
    CLOWN. CLOWN LOVE!
OHHHHHHHHHHHHHHHOOOOO
    OOOOOOOOOOUUUUUUUUUUUUUUU!!!!

YOUR LIPS – ARE THE BEST CLOWN LIPS I HAVE EVER
    KISSED
YOUR HIPS – ARE THE BEST CLOWN HIPS I HAVE EVER
    MISSED
YOUR EYES – SPARKLE IN THE NIGHT
LIKE A NIGHT – THIS ONE NIGHT – WHERE EV'RYTHING
    SPARKLES THAT NIGHT
CLOWN LOVE! IT'S LOVE BETWEEN A CLOWN AND A
    CLOWN. CLOWN LOVE!
OHHHHHHHHHHHHHHHOOOOO
    OOOOOOOOOOUUUUUUUUUUUUUUU!!!!

YOUR JUGS – ARE THE BEST CLOWN JUGS I HAVE EVER
    RUBBED
YOUR LOVE – IS THE BEST CLOWN LOVE I HAVE EVER
    LOVED
YOUR EYES – SPARKLE IN THE NIGHT
THIS ONE NIGHT – WHERE EV'RYTHING SPARKLES THAT
    NIGHT

CLOWN LOVE! IT'S LOVE BETWEEN A CLOWN AND A
    CLOWN. CLOWN LOVE!
OHHHHHHHHHHHHHHHOOOOO
    OOOOOOOOOOUUUUUUUUUUUUUUU!!!!

OOO

(The song ends. **GUSTY** *exits.* **POPO** *re-enters.*
*(***PETUNIA** *enters, leading* **TWINKLES**, *who is*
already bloody. Maybe she pulls him by the
hair or his ear or pushes him in at gunpoint.)

TWINKLES. Please. Petunia!

PETUNIA. Shut up! *(Maybe she slaps him.)* What are the coppers still doing here?

POPO. Soaking in the ambience.

PETUNIA. Getting ambience all over the bar.

TWINKLES. Help me.

GLORIA. We don't see nothing.

PETUNIA. You think you're clowns now?

MAC. No. I don't know.

PETUNIA. If you don't go now, you can't go at all. Go on, back to your beige life. You know what the clown bar life is.

MAC. So many dead clowns.

GLORIA. We'll go.

TWINKLES. Don't go. Wait!

PETUNIA. Thanks for your help.

> *(Exit* **MAC** *and* **GLORIA**, *maybe taking off noses and wigs as they go.)*

Twink, you done us wrong.

TWINKLES. I was just thinking of the bar.

PETUNIA. You was his friend.

TWINKLES. I know. I know you loved him. We all did. It's just.

POPO. No.

TWINKLES. I want an open casket, just don't shoot me in the face.

> *(***PETUNIA*** raises the gun. She closes her eyes. Beat. Beat. She hasn't shot him. He runs and ducks behind a table. He pulls out a gun and starts shooting.* **POPO** *and* **PETUNIA** *return fire. Enter* **GUSTY**.*)*

GUSTY. Hey, what you guys doing?

> (**GUSTY** *gets shot and dies.*)

PETUNIA. Aww.

POPO. Eh.

PETUNIA. I fucked up, Popo.

POPO. Just shoot him.

TWINKLES. You don't have to forgive me. I get it. But maybe you could just forget.

PETUNIA. Never.

> (**PETUNIA** *does the move* **POPO** *did earlier and sneaks up on* **TWINKLES** *and slits his throat or shoots him. Like a slide or a somersault. It's pretty fucking awesome.* **TWINKLES** *dies.*)

POPO. That works.

PETUNIA. Well, that's done.

POPO. I found Happy's nose. It rolled under the desk.

> (**POPO** *hands the nose to* **PETUNIA.** *Reverently, she puts it on. If she's already wearing a nose, she switches it out. She looks up into the light.*)

What now, boss?

End of Play

PRESHOW SONGS

"PETUNIA"

THERE'S A LITTLE FLOWER I WANT YOU TO MEET
A LOVELY TART WHO'S JUST SO SWEET
A DICKS IN VIXEN, ALL WAYS UP FOR MIXIN'
LET ME CROON YA 'BOUT PETUNIA

PETUNIA WILL NOON YA
PETUNIA WILL AFTERNOON YA
PETUNIA WILL SCREWN YA

PETUNIA PETUNIA
PETUNIA PETUNIA

THERE'S A LITTLE FLOWER I WANT YOU TO MEET
A SALTY TRICK WHO'S ALSO A TREAT
A DICKS IN VIXEN, ALL WAYS UP FOR MIXIN'
LET ME CROON YA ABOUT PETUNIA

PETUNIA WILL MOON YA
PETUNIA WILL SPOON YA
PETUNIA WILL MOCTEZUMYA

PETUNIA PETUNIA
SHE'LL SEE RIGHT THROUGHN YA
PETUNIA

PETUNIA FOUND RELIGION ON THE BACK OF A BIKE
UNDER THE COLLAR OF A MINISTER'S WIFE
IN THE SHOWER WITH MOST OF THE MEN FROM THE
    COAST
S'POSE THEY KNOWS WHY PETUNIA GLOWS?

THERE'S A LITTLE FLOWER, GLAD I HAD YOU GREET
A RACEY WENCH WHO'LL PACK YOUR MEAT

A DICKS IN VIXEN, ALL WAYS UP FOR MIXIN'
LET ME CROON YA 'BOUT PETUNIA

PETUNIA WILL RUIN YA
PETUNIA WILL RUIN YA
PETUNIA WILL RUIN YA

PETUNIA
PETUNIA PETUNIA

THERE'S NO ONE LIKE PETUNIA

"HAPPY"

HAPPY WAS A CLOWN
WASN'T HAPPY AS A CLOWN
WHEN WE WENT FROM TOWN TO TOWN,
HE WOULD CRY

AIN'T A LIFE FOR MEN
CIRCUS YOUR ONLY FRIEND
BROKEN FENCES COULDN'T MEND
HE WOULD CRY

CLOWNING LIFE IS BAD,
HARDEST LIFE I EVER HAD
HAPPY GOT TO FEELIN' SAD
HE WOULD CRY

One time, I remember
It was July or December
Just finishin' up a show
How they laughed, oh how they laughed
Then we left, and we cried
It wasn't funny. We drank a lot. Woke up angry.
Clowning ain't easy and neither is this song.
Will you button up that shirt please?

CLOWNING LIFE IS BAD,
HARDEST LIFE I EVER HAD
HAPPY GOT TO FEELIN' SAD

HE WOULD CRY

HAPPY WAS A CLOWN
WASN'T HAPPY AS A CLOWN
WHEN WE WENT FROM TOWN TO TOWN,
HE WOULD CRY
HE WOULD CRY
BOY, WOULD HE CRY

Never stopped crying.

"YOU'RE NOT WELCOME"

WHAT ARE YOU DOING HERE?
DRINKING ALL THIS CLOWNY BEER?
ENJOYING OUR ATMOSPHERE?
YOU'RE NOT A CLOWN

I'VE NEVER SEEN YOU HERE BEFORE.
NOT A GANGSTER OR A WHORE.
NOT EVEN FUNNY, YOU'RE A BORE.
YOU'RE NOT A CLOWN.

WHO TOLD YOU TO COME?
DRINK ALL OUR RUM.
YOU'RE JUST A BUM.
YOU'RE NOT A CLOWN.

YOU'RE NOT WELCOME.
YOU'RE NOT WELCOME.

It's just a song. You're totally welcome.

YOU'RE NOT WELCOME.
GET OUT OF HERE NOW.

You're totally welcome, thanks for coming.

YOU'RE NOT WELCOME AT ALL.

WHAT ARE YOU DOING HERE?
DRINKING ALL THIS CLOWNY BEER?
ENJOYING OUR ATMOSPHERE?

YOU'RE NOT A CLOWN

I HATE YOU A LOT.
JUST A DIRTY SNOT.
BREATHING ALL THE AIR WE GOT.
YOU'RE NOT A CLOWN.

I WISH YOU WOULD DIE.
GET ON YOUR BROOMSTICK AND FLY.
DON'T BOTHER SAYING BYE.
YOU'RE NOT A CLOWN.

YOU'RE NOT WELCOME.
YOU'RE NOT WELCOME.

It's just a song. You're totally welcome.

YOU'RE NOT WELCOME.
GET OUT OF HERE NOW.

You're totally welcome here.

YOU'RE NOT WELCOME AT ALL.
AT ALL.
AT ALL!

Thank you for coming.

"COULROPHOBIA"

COULROPHOBIA
FEAR OF CLOWNS ALL OVER YA
THEY'LL COME TO KILL YOU WHILE YOU'RE TRYING TO
    SLEEP
COULROPHOBIA
CLOWN FEAR CORNUCOPIA
THEY'LL MEET TO EAT YOU WHEN YOU'RE COUNTING
    SHEEP

CLOWNS ARE SUPER SCARY
THERE ARE MANY REASONS WHY
THEY'LL CHOP YOU UP WITH CLEAVERS

JUST TO EAT YOUR PIE
IF YOU LOOK AT THEM FUNNY
OR LOOK THEM IN THE EYE
THEY'LL CUT OFF YOUR FACE
AND COVER IT UP WITH LYE

COULROPHOBIA
FEEL THAT WAVE COME OVER YA
THEY'LL COME TO KILL YOU WHILE YOU'RE TRYING TO
    SLEEP
COULROPHOBIA
CLOWN FEAR EUPHORIA
THEY'LL MEET TO EAT YOU WHEN YOU'RE COUNTING
    SHEEP

IF YOU'RE NEAR A CLOWN,
DON'T EVER TAKE A CHANCE
DON'T WHISPER 'BOUT HIS SISTER,
OR ASK A CLOWN TO DANCE
DON'T TALK ABOUT THE WEATHER,
OR ABOUT HER BREAST ENHANCE
YOU'LL END UP IN THE OCEAN
WEARING CONCRETE PANTS

You should be afraid.
There's nothing scarier in this world
Than an angry clown,
Looking for blood...
Except a jealous clown.
Or a happy clown.
Or a thoughtful clown,
Or a wistful clown,
Or a clown just come from the dentist

COULROPHOBIA
FEEL THAT WAVE COME OVER YA
THEY'LL COME TO KILL YOU WHILE YOU'RE TRYING TO
    SLEEP

COULROPHOBIA
CLOWN FEAR EUPHORIA
THEY'LL MEET TO EAT YOU WHEN YOU'RE COUNTING
    SHEEP!

"CLOWNS UNDERCOVER!!"

YOU KNOW IT! YOU SAW IT!
THE SPACE IN THE BASEMENT
THEY HIDE IN THE CUPBOARD.
THEY HIDE IN THE FLOOR.
YOU KNOW IT! CONFRONT IT!
THE PLACE WHERE THE FACE WENT.
THEY'RE IN THERE! THEY'RE OUT THERE!
BOARD UP THE DOOR!!!

'CAUSE ONCE THEY COME IN HERE
THERE'S NO WAY TO STOP THEM.
THEY DON'T LISTEN TO REASON,
DON'T LISTEN TO RHYME.
THEY ARE KNOCKING YOU OVER.
THEY ARE PUSHING YOU UNDER.
THIS TIME THEY WILL GET YOU.
THEY'LL GET YOU THIS TIME.

YOU KNOW IT! YOU SAW IT!
THE SPACE IN THE BASEMENT
WHY DIDN'T YOU LISTEN?
I TOLD YOU THE SCORE.
YOU KNEW IT! YOU SAW IT!
THE PLACE WHERE THE FACE WENT.
THE CLOWNS ARE ALL COMING,
RIGHT THROUGH THE DOOR.
ONE! TWO! THREE! FOUR!

CLOWNS UNDERCOVER!!!
CLOWNS UNDERCOVER!!!

'CAUSE NOW THAT THEY'RE IN HERE,

THERE'S NO WAY TO STOP THEM.
THEY'RE LICKING YOUR GIRLFRIEND,
THEY'RE DRINKING YOUR WINE.
THEY ARE KNOCKING YOU OVER.
THEY ARE PUSHING YOU UNDER.
THIS TIME THEY'LL CONSUME YOU,
THEY'LL CONSUME YOU THIS TIME.

CLOWNS UNDERCOVER!!!
CLOWNS UNDERCOVER!!!
THEY'LL CONSUME YOU THIS TIME!